FANTASY SEX COLLECTION
EXPLICIT DIRTY EROTICA SHORT STORIES

MACKENZIE HARNDEN

plicit Press

CHAPTER 1

BATHED IN MOONLIGHT

NINETEEN-YEAR-OLD MIA DAHL had spotted her mark. On the other side of the bonfire, her best friend was on the prowl. Iani Belle was also nineteen; both girls celebrated their birthdays just two weeks before. Being the only surviving heirs for their respective packs, the girls had always been inseparable. Even now, as they were hunting, they were aware of the other one.

Mia struck first. The college soccer star had been eyeing her from the moment she'd arrived at the party. His white-blond hair and hazel eyes had half the female attention from the start. At first, Mia had ignored him, searching for a loner, but something about him kept drawing her back. The wolf inside her stirred and she knew her time was growing short. She needed to fuck, and soon.

She sauntered towards him, every inch of her athletic body roiling with power. Her long walnut brown hair swayed freely and her eyes, the same deep brown as the earth, glowed with an unearthly light. The moment her gaze met his, he was entranced. Out of the corner of her eye, she saw Iani leading a young man with caramel-colored hair and ice gray eyes into the woods. Mia could feel the were-leopard princess's energy from the distance. The moon was calling them both.

Mia took James's hand and slid it up under her camisole to her small breast. She didn't have the time to be subtle. The expression on his face would've been comical if she hadn't been so desperate.

Less than five minutes later, Mia was on her knees, mouth working around James's cock. It swelled as she sucked, hollowing out her cheeks until he moaned. She ran her tongue along the underside, pulling her head back until it fell from between her lips. She kept one hand wrapped around the shaft, a slow, steady rhythm going as she stood. James stared at her, pupils blown wide as if he weren't entirely sure of the reality of what was happening. Mia turned to face a large pine, glancing over her shoulder at her gaping partner.

"Fuck me," Mia flipped up her short skirt, revealing her total lack of anything underneath. "Shit," James fumbled with his zipper for a moment before pausing to speak. "I don't have a condom."

Mia growled in frustration, hearing her beast in the tones. "I'm clean and on the pill. Just fuck me already." The lie didn't matter as long as the results were the same. Weres didn't get STDs, didn't really get diseases of any kind actually, and they could only breed with another of their kind. No such thing as half-breeds in the Were world.

He shoved inside her, long and hard and almost too fast. Mia whimpered at the burn as he stretched her more quickly than was entirely pleasant. The bark cut into her palms as she pushed back against him, forcing him deep enough for a spark of pain to flare through her. Her eyes flashed to the russet of her wolf, body responding immediately to the jolt, going rigid as she climaxed. She cried out, letting her body absorb the sensations as James continued to pump into her, the tip of him bumping against the end of her. Each shock sent another orgasm through her and nudged her beast that much closer to the surface. She needed him to cum. She flexed her muscles, squeezing his cock until he exploded inside her with a drawn-out groan.

She heard Iani and her companion before she saw them. Her nose flared the scent of sex and nature heavy in the air. Mia stepped into the clearing and leaned back against a tree, with no trace of embarrassment or self-consciousness as she watched her friend. They'd been hunting together for years, had shared and swapped partners, and even had the occasional threesome. The leopards and wolves worked together so well in large part to the relationship between the two girls.

Iani's copper curls had recently been cropped short, framing the heart-shaped face currently wearing an expression of pure bliss. Though her eyes were closed, Mia knew they'd be as green as the grass beneath the girl's hands and knees. If her beast were ready to emerge, shots of pure gold would shoot through the green.

"Harder, Owen," Iani was nearly purring as the man behind her snapped his hips forward with even more force. Mia could tell from the angle and the way the were-leopard was writhing that the young man Iani had called Owen was fucking her ass. Mia's stomach clenched, desire flaring again. "So tight," Owen grunted the sheen of sweat on his forehead visible to Mia's supernatural eyes.

"I want to go inside you."

Mia slid her hand under her skirt, fingers instantly slick with her own juices as they passed between her folds. Dark eyes traced the elegant lines of Iani's lithe body, taking in the girl's arched back, the snaking beneath her, working between her legs even as Mia did the same. The wereleopard's breathing quickened, signaling her impending orgasm. Mia recognized the sound and slipped two fingers into her pussy, the cum from her previous encounter still dripping. She pressed the heel of her hand against her clit.

"Fuck," Owen cried out as he came, hips stuttering against Iani's ass.

The sound that came from Iani's mouth as her body convulsed with the force of her climax could only be described as a yowl. Her body shuddered, skin rippling as she fought back her beast. That sound alone made Mia cum again, pleasure coursing through her body, waves washing over her even as her beast stretched and squirmed beneath the surface.

The moon was too close to its peak, too close to the point where all Weres, wolf and leopard alike, would be forced to turn. They needed to leave.

"We have to go," Mia straightened, pulling her skirt back down. She crossed to Iani on shaky legs, ignoring the startled exclamation from the young man sprawled on the forest floor. Iani rolled onto her back, a satisfied grin on her full lips.

"Iani, now," Mia extended a hand.

· · ·

The other girl sighed and let Mia pull her upright. The wereleopard tugged her dress back into place. "Yeah, you're right. I can feel it." Iani glanced up at the darkening sky before dropping her eyes back down to Owen.

"Did he have enough to drink?" Mia asked.

Iani nodded. "He'll barely remember that he fucked someone, let alone who." As if to prove her point, Owen slumped back to the ground, eyes fluttering closed as he passed out.

"Let's go," Mia took her friend's hand and the pair ran deeper into the woods, up towards where they'd arranged to meet their packs. Where they would shift and spend the rest of the night in their other form, roaming the mountains under the pale light of the full moon.

CHAPTER 2

FLYING THE WINGS OF LOVE

FLYING TOWARD HER, I didn't know if it was a dream or real. She was a beautiful girl with a pageboy black hair-cut, nice heavy tits, and wide thirty-two-inch hips. How I flew baffled me; but frankly, I didn't care. She had gorgeous pink downy wings fluttering from just under her shoulder blades and my clit thrummed insistently for her touch. We flew in the blue skies high above the earth. We soared above the sun and outer space in this place she called Haven Groove.

We embraced in mid-air, instantly turning my nips into hard pebbles. I closed my eyes and kissed her softly. I ran one hand down her flat belly toward her snatch. Her pubic hair's softness made me horny and freed my spirit with wild abandon. She grasped one of my tits in her small hands and raised it to her mouth. She had cherry red lips. No makeup. Just those cherry red lips that tasted like sweet preserves. I spread my legs. I dipped two fingers into her and stroked her heated core. As she became more aroused, she fluttered her pink wings harder and harder. We flew higher and higher!

My skin increased in sensitivity the higher we lifted into Haven Groove. She rolled me over in the weightless air as if I were a dandelion drifting. On top of me, she pressed her cherry lips to my swollen nipples. She sucked and bit my nipples. Her tit did this wonderful pulling-scraping dance over my nips. Sometimes I wanted to push her mouth away hard. When the pain grew too intense and harsh my Angel Girl slathered and bathed my tit-flesh using her soft wet tongue.

"You're my dream girl," she cooed as we dove down toward the faraway sun. The swift breeze cooled our damp skin. The air rushing past fluffed my cunt hairs.

"Feel the air making love to your skin," she said. "Relax. I have you in my arms."

My Angel Girl allowed me to indulge in every sensual fantasy. This had to be a dream. I loved her and her attentiveness to my every need, inside and out.

She smiled. "My name is Herais," she said, and added, "Are you ready for more?"

I panted yes. I batted my eyelids to match her eyelash flirting. She began using her gentle tongue. Then she pushed me away. Helpless I fell downward. She watched me fall away.

. . .

Then she rushed back toward me and scooped me into her long arms. She twisted her body around and we formed a 69. My sopping hole lapped at her jabbing tongue. I dug my fingers into her ivory buns and mashed my face into her snatch, kissing, licking, drowning her labes with my hot tongue.

She reacted by arching her back and moaning loud. "I love your Haven Groove."

That's when I knew this could not be a masturbation dream. This was no masturbation fantasy I had before drifting off to sleep like I did every night. She was real. I was trembling. I was too excited to control my pussy folds from quaking under her expert tongue's stirring. We came in unison, our moans blocked out the rushing air as we flew upward into the sky!

Her pussy smelled like pineapples and primroses. I loved her fruity scent. It lingered on my tongue as we turned around to face one another again, lazily drifting sideways. I wanted some place to put her down. On a striped, beach chair, a white sofa, maybe a kitchen table. Any place where my sole focus narrowed on her wet cunt. "I want to suck your cunt. I want to embrace your creamy ivory thighs and bury my head between your angelic legs."

She understood.

.   .   .

She embraced my elbow and flew me downward until we reached a big soft cloud. The Queen- sized cloud drifted gently in the wind. She lay on her back. I knelt between her outstretched legs and the cloud adjusted lowering me until my mouth fit her pussy perfectly. I wrapped my arms under the twin peaks of her bent legs. My hands caressed her belly button and her Venus mound. The Angel Girl let out a peal of laughter.

"Your French kissing tongue drives me wild with lust." She reached under my face and spread her lips wide. Her glistening cunt lips revealed her pearly clit. Immediately, I licked my tongue around her clit and slurped it into my mouth. Pursing my lips, I held her clit for a few seconds. I released it. I sucked it back into my mouth, held it, and released it. I tried a third time, but her little pearl quivered so much, it was impossible to catch it as the Angel Girl screamed out loud and forced my mouth on top of her cunt.

Herais forcefully held my mouth to her heated sex. Her labia lips licked and sucked on my face and tongue. Liberally she spewed her girly juices all over my face. I moved my fingers back under her hips, found her opening, and stuffed two of my fingers inside. She humped my fingers, swallowing them into her. She wanted more; so I twisted my hand until my thumb made tight circles around her clit. She writhed in my arms for even more.

So I took my other thumb and stuffed it gently up her bum hole. I wished my fingers were longer, like hers. I wanted to reach deep into her sex. I settled for rapid in and out movements teasing and stroking her entire pelvic floor until she burst into the most magical song as her multi-orgasm overtook her being.

I'll never forget that song. Herais' Song. Every night I hum it as I masturbate thinking, dreaming to see my Angel Girl again. And I always come waiting for her to return and lift me away from the gravity of the earth and into Haven Groove's weightless sky.

CHAPTER 3

FOREST FEVER

IF IT WASN'T for her strength, the result of having to do everything for herself around her home deep in the dark forests of the bayou, Nala, a voodoo high priestess, would never have been able to carry the large-framed Negro into her house. Why he had strayed so far was not clear, but his shorts and vest let her know that he had not intended to get lost in the middle of nowhere. But he had been burning up with a fever and so she had brought him home to use her magic to treat him. But the beautiful brown body on the floor in front of her was not responding as she had hoped.

She was getting worried.

The sweat glistened on every part of him, the candle-light flickering and licking the drops with orange glows. Nala lifted her skirt and tucked it in at the waist as she prepared herself to intensify her efforts. Her hands were a dark red from the mixture she had manufactured to rub into the man and her hands moved over his thick arms and around his neck. He didn't stir, just produced more and more salty beads from the parts of himself that she touched. Nala moved her hands under his vest, his chest, and his perfectly sculpted abs. Wherever he comes from and whatever it is that he does there, this man is all about fitness. But he has no response to her touch, or to her medicine. He just keeps getting better, his nipples getting harder.

Strange warmth travels through her now as she touches him. The heat comes from him, and also from her. She notices his face now, its beauty, its strength, and finds herself moving her fingers over it. Her hands settle on his cheeks and then without thinking, Nala is kissing him. His lips are full and soft and she kisses them for a long time. She wants to taste the contents of his mouth and so she sends her tongue into it. Nala almost doesn't expect to be let in but her tongue is instantly inside him, and on his tongue. She lets her tongue play with his, hoping for a response, anything to let her know that he is aware of her. There is no response.

Her kissing intensifies and her hand moves down his chest and onto his crotch. The hard cock that she finds there lets her know that at least he is aware of himself. This is a good sign. Without thinking too much she unwraps the cock, removing the shorts and covering it with a large pair of scissors. She removes his vest the same way. A moment later Nala has the most beautiful chocolate log in her hands. His cock is long and thick. It has the kind of hardness that lets her know that were the owner awake, it would be a pretty powerful piece of equipment. She wishes more than ever now that he would just wake up. With one hand on the cock she desires, she lets her other hand attend to her cunt, now caught in a fever of its own. She touches herself hard, imagining what it might feel like to be touched by the man with the escalating temperature before her.

Nala lets go of the cock she now wants and lets the fingers on her now free hand join her other in her cunt.

Very carefully she coats each and every one of her fingers with the contents of her pussy. Then both her hands are on the boner again, her cunt left to beat alone to its own drum.

She works her hands over the meat with great care to provide as much pleasure as possible. She hopes that where magic has failed primal lust might succeed. The inside of her thighs starts to drip from the contents of her cunt that flows down onto them. The sweat between her legs fuses with her lust and she is soon as wet on the outside as she is on the inside. Again she wishes that this man with such potential to take her on an unbelievable ride would just wake up. But the only parts of him that seem to live are his nipples, his cock, and his balls.

Needing to be naked with him, Nala removes all her own clothes. Her tongue rests on his chest and then finds his nipples, giving each of them a generous amount of licking and an even more generous amount of sucking. His cock is on his stomach, lying way past his naval pointing in the direction of his chest. She sandwiches his thick sausage with her own belly, his balls in the warm cove formed by her cunt and her thighs brought tightly together. Sucking on his nipples she rubs her pussy in gentle ovals against the base of his penis. His cock is so stimulated that it pushes up against her tummy hard as if to lift her off of itself. She realizes the power of the tool and her cunt flows in its absolute desire for this cock now.

Nala tastes his lips again. She kisses him and then sends her tongue into his warm mouth again. To her surprise, he starts to kiss her back. She opens her eyes and looks at his. His are still closed. But his mouth has come to life and their tongues are locked in fire and passion. Then her one thigh is covered with fingers, then the other. Both her thighs are held in firm hands and then lifted. This move bends her knees, her pussy open wide. Suddenly the man under her is very present. He slides her up over his chest so that her cunt moves an inch above where the end of his cock is. Then he positions her on his cock before sliding her back down on it. Her wet cunt covers the cock completely as it works its way down to the base.

She can't bring herself to look at him now, embarrassed that she had touched him before he was awake. She can't be sure now that he is awake but since he's taken control of her body she has to believe that he is. Whatever her experience with the dark magic has taught her, she won't let herself question what is happening to her now, her body wanting it too much. Again she is sliding up the cock, and then back down onto it. Up the fifteen-inch shaft her cunt travels, the thickness of it filling her as much up as wide. The slide down is a mix of slow pushes followed by longer more fluid strokes. Each time she is right at the base of the cock, taking every throbbing inch into her tight cunt. Her breasts are on his hard nipples throughout.

Then a massive force from below as the cock is pushed up into her while her cunt is held down. The dick seems to fly through the air, taking her pussy with it despite the resistance from his hands on her ass. The wooden floor creeks loudly beneath them as Nala is lifted high up through her vagina, kept in mid-air for a split second, and then brought back down. She herself adds to the reach of the cock by pushing herself down onto it too. The feeling of the strong hands on her ass, controlling and moving her, makes her want to give him more of herself, as much as possible. There is no part of his cock that isn't acquainted with her cunt.

Her purple clit grazes beautifully against him. Her vagina strains against the cock that seems to be gaining girth now the more rampant his ramming. The fucking becomes an intense feeding frenzy, the cock inside her and its owner seeming to go absolutely crazy as her pussy becomes soaked in fluid. The wetness, the slippery feel of the tight hole sees it fucked harder and harder now that the movement both in and out of it seems to be freer. Suddenly the man, his fever broken but the sweat still flowing, sits up and then is on top of Nala. She has no time to move, process, or make any other decision as the cock finds her g-spot and hits it in such quick succession that even the orgasm she was about to have suddenly pauses.

The darkest, deepest eyes look down on her, just as the cock hits her spot again. There's a look of total control, total satisfaction. The cock pulls her cunt from its position and then puts it back. It seems to remove layers of pleasure from within her and then replenish the pleasure store a hundred-fold each time it drills back into her. With the complete weight of him on top of her, Nala feels as though he is digging her hole a little deeper. It feels like his power drill might shoot right through her at any second. The thought is scary, arousing the princess of dark magic immensely. He ploughs into her with such force that the floor beneath them is at risk of giving way, the creaking unbelievably loud now.

Her legs form a V as he splits them above her head and to the side. His cock now moves so completely into her with absolutely zero restriction now. The entire tool falls into her and lifts out of her amidst the warm wetness. Her feet touch the wood for the force of his push. The fucking elevates and then escalates, moving Nala through worlds invisible. She's seldom so completely pleasured that she has an out-of-body experience. This is, fortunately, such a time. Her vagina becomes a pulsating oven around the cock that seems both unaffected by her heat and inspired by it.

Their bodies slide over one another for all the sweating,

but thanks to his cock, the connection is never lost. The fevered stranger fucks her feverishly now as the possibility of climax dawns. It is Nala who flows first, her pussy banging against every inch of the cock as its fire peaks. The cock moves rapidly in and out of her as it too starts to peak. Their orgasms merge and the floor takes most of the shock of the impact, its loud creaking absorbing their moans as well. It starts to thunder loudly outside and immediately the rain comes down hard. It takes four more rounds for the now fever-free midnight man to appease his cock, and with his fever broken, he finally leaves Nala in a satisfied mess on her floor.

The night is filled with visions of dark cock and sweat which are a mix of waking dreams and vivid memories. Nala knows that it will probably be some time before she has another such experience and so she is in no hurry to pull herself together. She lets her mind take her where it wills, and her body follows, a willing slave to her lusts. Her fingers treat her pussy to tender touches that leave her dripping repeatedly until finally, she loses herself to sleep.

CHAPTER 4

FUCKING FOR MOTHER EARTH

THE FIVE OF us wanted to be earth mothers, just like those ancient Venus of Willendorf statues. We wanted to feel loved and needed. Each of us lay on our backs on a small white twin bed. Each at the foot of the bed, curled up. Our elbows were hooked behind the back of our knees. Our wrists are tied by rope to our ankles. Naked. Exposed we waited, a ball gag in some of our mouths. I didn't want a ball gag in my mouth, because I love to moan and make all kinds of sexual noises.

The men loved to fuck the earth mother, the madam told us. "You don't have to worry about being selected. When they look through the window, it will be like looking at a museum. All they will see is your asshole and gaping wet pussy hole waiting for someone to enter. Waiting for someone to accept their manly seeds." I had been lying there on the small twin bed for ten minutes. The other four women chose to wear ball gags. They didn't want the men to be turned off in any way.

.   .   .

I said, "You think they're making us wait here on purpose?"

"Mmm-hmmm," said the girl to the far right of me. Gloria wore a red ball gag.

"Hmmm-hmmm," responded the second girl on my near left. Kitty wore a white ballgag. "Uuuhmmm," replied, the third girl near on my right. Sheena's mouth held a yellow ball gag. "Ahhhhh," said, the fourth girl to the far left of me. Wendy's ball gag was black.

"Well at least, you're coming, Wendy." She was a wavy brunette with small tits. "And Sheena, you too, sound like an orgasm is close at hand."

Gloria wore a red ball gag and she kept circling her hips trying to fuck herself using her large inner labes that spilled over on her outer labia lips. She had platinum straight hair.

Kitty's bed squeaked as she used her elbows to massage her own floppy tits.

A voice came over the loudspeaker. "The Ghost from Atlantis will be visiting you, ladies, shortly."

.   .   .

All of us heated up. The small bedroom smelled like musky earth on a wet and rainy day. Being horny and exposed like that for ten minutes kept our fantasies firing and rewinding and replaying again and again.

Finally, the door whined and opened slowly. Each of us raised our heads to look. "Nnmmmuuunnmm-Nmmm!" Murmured Kitty under her white ball gag.

"Nommmmooom--Nummmm!" Shenna shook her head violently, under her yellow ball gag. "Ahhhhhh!" Murmured Wendy. Her black ballgag protruding in and out like she was trying to fuck her mouth.

"Lmmmmmmuuuuumm!" Murmured Gloria mewed under her red ball gag.

What we saw horrified us and excited us at the same time. One man came into the room attached to another in a long white transparent shape. Each man, although shaped like a normal human, only had his arms linked to the other men. From their lower loins jutted cocks anywhere from six inches to nine inches long. But that wasn't what horrified us. Each of the five ghostly men flashed all sorts of long tentacles growing and shrinking from their skin. From their torsos grew long appendages curved and round at the tip. Even the men's nipples pushed out long tubular flesh and stretched out toward our open orifices.

I now wished I had worn a ball gag.

Each man stood in front of us. Before I could react, the Ghost from Atlantis oozed out his appendages from his nipples. His nipple being on the front end of the appendage and wrapped itself around both my DD boobies. That long appendage felt cool to the touch but slick and slippery like silicone lubricant. My tits purred as the appendage finished looping around and his extended nipple stretched out and started to kiss my nipples! Our nipples were kissing! The swollen nubs on my chest kept going up and down as the appendage squeezed. I moaned out and came right away. I tried to catch my breath only to find the Ghost from Atlantis stuffing his seven-inch, fireplug cock up my wet slot. I stopped all movement as his dick pushed restlessly inside my cunt. "Ohhh that feels good! More. More!" He kept fucking me as another limb of his pressed out from the small of his back. It had to be because I couldn't see it. It was like a thick quarter-inch tail, and it thrashed around my gurgling pussy hole wetting itself before he plunged into my asshole.

I saw stars and more stars. The cool appendage in my asshole twisted and twirled really fast; so fast I forgot all about my pure fuck slit. But my Ghost Atlantis man didn't. His navel pushed out into a string-thin line and slid up my inner labia until he reached the hood of my clit. My pearl quivered in her juices. I fought back from coming. "No, wait! Not yet!"

Too late, that string-like cool appendage slipped inside my clitoral hood and wrapped itself around my stub of a clit, and started jerking the thing off like it was a tiny cock. The pale ghost man wore a wicked smile on his face. The corners of his lip showed his bent tongue, drooling ready to come out somewhere. I didn't know where. I tried to listen. I heard Kitty's bed squeaking like a gymnast used it as a trampoline. Before two more cool appendages plugged up my ears. I was sure Sheena came. Gloria shrieked. Kitty purred. Wendy's ball gag was somehow removed by her Ghost Atlantis Man and she said, "I'm going to finally cum!" something muffled her again.

I soon found out what. My Ghost Atlantis Man's cool appendage slipped inside my mouth. My gag reflex started. His long tubular limbs squirted some slippery goo down my throat and stopped it. I don't know what it was, but it felt good sucking on his appendage as it slithered down my throat and back out again. I rolled my tongue around his blue appendage and tried to hold on to no avail. My Ghost Man fucked me in every hole available. He even managed to slip a tiny appendage into my piss hole and I felt only immense pleasure. I fainted several times only to be revived by the Atlantis Ghost Man pulling out and shooting his blue jism all over my face, up to my nose a bit. My short dark hair looked more salt and pepper by the time I was released by the Madam. She assured me the Ghost Men of Atlantis would love to fuck me again. And asked, "Echo do you want to come back?"

I hesitated then said, "Sure if the same Ghost Man from Atlantis wants me I'll return!" The Madam assured me he wanted to fuck me again. Fuck me again in every way.

So I signed the Whorehouse Agreement and look forward to fucking him again.

CHAPTER 5

RESCUED BY THE SEX PRINCESS

THE DRAGON LASHED OUT ONCE MORE. His fiery breath took away my beard. Now I was as clean-shaven as a youth of sixteen. I pulled my fireproof black cape around me and pressed forward, slashing at his scales. He growled low and curled back before tossing a large diamond bauble at my chest. I didn't have time to dodge, only to deflect it off my silver Shield of Truth. The diamond crashed into the wall and I saw the first glimmer of a treasure richer than all the wealth of a city paved in gold, Princess Eculine!

Eculine huddled in her long white gown, slit up the side to reveal her black skimpy thong. I wanted to fuck her right away...only the Dragon had other intentions. He flapped his large wings and raised high above the chandelier in the cave vault. The twinkling lights blinded me. When the continuous noise of the chandelier stopped twinkling and shaking, the dragon's green and white checked scales covered the jagged gap in the wall. He lowered his head and his eyes narrowed, shooting real darts out. Carefully, I lifted my feet and twisted my arms and body behind my shield. I hopped as the darts aimed at my feet stuck to the floor and oozed acid that began melting the cave floor.

Eculine screamed, "Help me!"

"I'm here my brave woman!" I crouched behind my shield and sped forward hoping to knock the Dragon over or lodge his tail into the small aperture in the wall. He caught me in his three-clawed hand and started squeezing the Shield of Truth on my front and against my steel helmet on my head. I kept trying to remember the words of the Witch who knew the Dragon's deadly secrets.

She said if you dedicate yourself with an open heart, the Dragon can no longer slay you.

"What did she mean?" I thought as my shield buckled, bending under the dull-ivory fingernails of the Dragon. My head began to ache from the pressure the monster exerted on my forehead.

Eculine's beautiful body did wonders for my imagination. How much fun to experience. If I saved her if I survived. She had the breasts like two ostrich eggs, round and perfectly spherical. Her hips spread out and pushed the splits of her skimpy white gown aside showing off her long luscious legs.

I yelled out a scream. "You will not stop me from mating and finding love!"

The Dragon stopped fighting. He released me and dropped me from five feet onto the ground. "Why didn't you say you loved Eculine before?" he huffed. "I'm only guarding her against false lovers and bad boys who meant to fuck her and dump her." The green and white dragon had a silver tear in his eyes.

I adjusted my warrior tunic over my gold-plated breeches. My iron boots clanked as I walked past the Dragon who bowed. "You may enter and find love."

I entered the jagged opening and stared in awe of Princess Eculine. "I'm in love. I want no one else but you forever."

"But can you fuck!" She sneered. "Usually guys who love are wimps in bed. If you fail to satisfy me, my Dragon shall surely do you in. So far, she's only toyed with you!" She pulled several silver rods in front of her buxom body. She encased herself in a cage.

She was built like an Amazon.

I tossed down my shield and unbuckled my shin guards. I pulled my red and black diamond tunic over my head. My sex jutted straight out. Precum dripped from the head of my stiff cock as I lowered my cotton-long underpants. I walked barefoot closer and closer to Princess Eculine.

The Dragon stuck his big head inside the small jagged opening. His large two eyes, lenses framing our intimate act.

I took Princess Eculine into my arms and kissed her gently at first. My hands slid like butter all over her body. I left not one inch of her skin untouched or caressed. I did magic between her legs and soon she ripped off her gauzy gown and lay back on the rich thick furs of bear, mink, and lion. She spread her legs and I lowered my tongue to taste her sex. I sucked the juices out of her dripping cunt. I teased her clit until she stood up and parted the apex of her sex. I placed my leg between her trembling needy thighs. I pressed my hard sex against her softness and entered in oneness.

Princess Eculine dragged me down and said, "I shall never leave this hole unless you're not afraid to wait to let me make love to you."

I had to think hard about this. Hard with both heads. "I climbed this steep mountain to bury my cock in you. I want your snatch to drip all over my penis."

She rolled me over and hovered her pussy over my dripping bloated cock head. All I wanted was for Princess Eculine to consummate the act. I dreamed of her wrapped around my lonely cock. She smiled wickedly before indulging me in my desires. As her firm, sexy cunt folds lowered and pushed outward over my engorged dick meat, I sighed. I melted under her. I gave in and allowed her to fuck me.

Eculine rose gently up and down, taking her sweet time in sending my dick to the back of her cunt. I simmered in her pussy hole as she showered me in ten thousand kisses. She made a way for me to achieve that singular unity of resting in her needs. She sat her ass on my thighs and slowly rode me like a cowgirl, trotting over the Great Plains. I settled into her rhythm and my scalding hot jism boiled for release. Finally, the jism held tight against my groin overflowed the top. My volcanic dickhead showered her cervix in my genetic pool material. A smile came on her face, and the Dragon cooed. I turned.

"She is a female Dragon," Eculine said. "You're surrounded by strong women, my fair knight.

"I don't care. I give in. I give up. I surrender to your love, Princess Eculine. Forever! Do with me what you want."

Eculine fucked me until my balls became like summer raisins. Devoid of man seeds, all I could do to satisfy her cunt-lust was roll out my tongue and taper it to lick her sloppy slit, until she came and screamed holding my two ears between her dripping thighs.

I can't say I rescued Eculine. But it sure feels good to lay back and let her fuck me before an audience of two.

CHAPTER 6

THE FAIRY QUEEN'S LUST (A MID-AFTERNOON FOREST FUCK)

THE AFTERNOON SUN has already warmed the sleeping warrior-elf's skin gently. But it's not the sun that now stirs his depths as he opens his eyes to find none other than the fairy-queen herself with his dick firmly between her fingers. He isn't sure whether to let her know that he is awake, the queen having uncovered his cock while he slept. He closes his eyes, deciding that if this was in fact a dream, it was still way too early to wake up. Remy, the warrior-elf, decides to snooze on when the queen's delicate tongue settles on the head of his already massive cock.

Elves have interesting dicks, a fact that the queen is aware of, but one she has not yet experienced firsthand. So this elf, a warrior no less, was an opportunity she was not going to pass up. In her hands the cock is rubbery, thick, and long. It seems to breathe as she touches, tugs, and licks it. With her hands on the shaft, it appears too thick for her mouth. But once she starts to lick the domed head, the dick seems to snake into her mouth of its own accord. Her mouth is quickly filled with the monster, which smells like sandal-wood but tastes conspicuously like vanilla. She enjoys the taste of the head, shaft, and even the large balls at the base of the breathing rubber rod.

Remy's balls, unlike his cock, are a consistent size. As her majesty licks the orbs, they move around in the warm soft sack that houses them. The two rounds are too large, even on their own, to fit completely in her tiny mouth and so all she can manage are licks. But her tongue morphs easily from delicate and gentle, to fucking powerful. As she licks over the entire surface of the sizable testicles, the cock just above them extends and shortens, thickens, and then gets thinner, beating in long whip-like strokes against the chiseled chest of the strange cock's owner. The queen takes the tool in hand and holds onto it while her licking continues to send it into a frenzy.

The one thing that everyone knows about an elf is that while they are not easily aroused, once you get them amorous, there is very little that will stop them from seeing the encounter through to an explosive end. This is great if you're an elf yourself and are able to fuck for at least twenty-four hours. If not, you might just be biting off more than you can chew. And the fairy- queen seems to be doing just that, Remy, no longer able to pretend to be asleep, taking her head in hand. He lifts her off his nuts and watches as his cock, all on its own, pushes through her grip and settles briefly on her lips before proceeding into her mouth. The fairy flutters off the ground but cannot get high enough fast enough and Remy's cock is quickly attached to the inside of her mouth. She can do nothing but suck on it as it expands to almost fill her mouth, and then contracts briefly to give her the space needed to breathe.

As her breasts bloom, swelling to perfect peaks in her light silk dress, Remy can't help but remove her from his cock and pull her down so that he takes her breasts into his mouth. The silk of her dress is almost edible, with scents and tastes of everything from jasmine to summer peaches fused into the fabric. The fairy hovers above him, her wings beating so rapidly that they disappear. Remy reaches up, pulls the part of the dress covering her breasts off, and then pulls the mounds into his waiting mouth. The queen's flesh is soft. It tastes like everything her dress alluded to and so Remy sucks on them as though he had the promise that these flavors might start to seep through the perfect nipples.

His cock goes crazy, stretching towards the queen's cunt, finding it. Remy has to keep moving his long dick away manually so as not to penetrate the queen prematurely. He knows from watching her responses to his cock's breathing, its stretching and its regular assumptions of independent life, that she has never been fucked by an elf. Remy is a warrior-elf. The queen cannot possibly know what she has set herself up for. Yes, fairy-men have large, thick, powerful cocks. But you know with them that what you see is what you get. With elves, it's a whole other story. Remy pulls the fairy-queen by the waist so that while she continues to flutter mid-air, her cunt is now in Remy's face. The elf is grateful that the queen of all the forest has no panties on.

Her cunt tastes like every fruit, but berries dominate. Remy has to do everything he can not to take a bite out of the tender pussy in his mouth. His tongue is inside the tight, tiny space quickly, the interior as tasty as the outside. The queen might have never been with an elf, but Remy too is having his first fairy *punani*. He is better at hiding his pleasant surprise though. Without skipping a beat, he eats out the fairy queen's pussy without once considering that it might be polite to say hello and formally introduce himself. Formalities are unimportant when sexualities are dominant.

Remy has held out as long as he can. It's time to get his dick inside her. She might not be able to handle it though, and the risk that he might be turned into a firefly or a toad enters his mind briefly. But his lust and the subsequent demands from his cock have him override anxiety and pull her majesty within cunt-reach of his cock. The rubbery length quickly extends in the direction of the pussy, Remy parting the fairy's legs and holding them open as her wings keep her airborne. His cock is at the entrance, elongating and thinning suddenly so that it makes an easy job of entering the tiny pussy. The cock snakes into the royal vagina quickly, the fairy- queen trying to elevate herself a little as the tip of the knob inside her reaches the extremities of her pussy. But Remy's grip on her legs is firm.

Her majesty's eyes fall on the cunt between her parted legs. Remy's eyes are on his cock in the cunt. The audience, a cautious distance away, watches the space where elf cock and fairy cunt connect, many of them aware of the rumors, excited for the possible confirmation. They all watch intently. For a minute, a very brief minute, nothing happens. But then the queen lets out a loud gasp, then a yelp. Everyone comes closer, ready to help her, to yank her from off of the elf. Remy's cock, once a thin rubber worm working its way gently into the cunt at its disposal, has now become a rapidly expanding rod forcing the fairy-queen's vaginal walls outward.

Realizing what is going on, the queen's wings beat almost as hard as her clit and she tries for the skies. Tiny tendrils immediately protrude from Remy's cock and attach to the inside of the queen's pussy, small suckers at the end of the tendrils making the grip an intense one. There seem to be millions of the tiny suckers and the queen is unable to move further than Remy's cock will allow. With the hot, flavored vagina now locked in place, Remy introduces the queen of all the fairy folk to the full measure of an elf cock.

His cock thickens to the point that the onlookers think the queen might explode from the internal pressure. The fairy-queen is having a totally different experience however, her vagina fucked by a single solid living dick, her walls tugged on by a million smaller dicks. She cannot venture an explanation to herself of the sensation, craving just that she were closer to the man fucking her. Sensing her desire, Remy wills his penis shorter to allow them to embrace. With the queen now in his arms, their lips locked, he continues fucking her, his dick fattening, beating, pulsating, but no longer lengthening. There is no build-up, no sense of an impending orgasm. The fairy-queen feels like she is lost in one long, dreamy, beautiful climax.

Suddenly the tendrils release and the cock makes a massive expansion before contracting to a manageable girth. The base of the cock grows alone now, a large round orb. Then the circle is inside the queen's vagina, too big almost for her tiny cunt as it travels slowly up the length of Remy's shaft. The queen holds tightly onto Remy as she realizes that the round expansion inside her is actually a ball moving up the inside of Remy's cock, and that this ball is about to be released inside her. Remy whispers into her ear that she should brace herself, and hold on. She does, not sure what it is she is bracing herself for other than the deposit of a ball too large for the inside of her vagina.

The orb is finally ejaculated, the penis immediately a little smaller. The orb dances around inside her for a minute and then attaches to the side of her vagina. Then, almost immediately, there is another orb at the base of her pussy. The orb moves up the shaft quicker, and then it too is deposited. Remy can't speak, kissing the queen on her neck and lips, occasionally her cheeks as he loses himself in his first orgasm. The orbs are released in rapid succession now, varying in size, the cock getting smaller and smaller with each orb that escapes it. The orbs, which everyone imagines to be glowing balls of white and silver light if the soft glow exuding from the queen is anything to go by. The last orb, just slightly larger than the current comfortable girth of Remy's cock makes its escape, and Remy pants on the queen's neck. She is about to move away from him, thinking mistakenly that since she's had several orgasms in the course of the orb deposits, that this tryst is over. Far from it though, Remy pulling her closer, holding her in place for what he knows is about to happen.

Suddenly the orbs start to explode inside the fairy-queen's cunt. Her vagina feels like it has just been soaked in popping candy and gallons of fizz as she experiences the most exhilarating sensation she has ever felt. Orb after orb explodes inside her, popping and fizzing, sending millions of stardust particles through the walls of her vagina, and all over her body. She glows brightly and then starts to sparkle as the product of Remy's pleasure introduces the fairy queen to her first elf-induced climax.

During this explosion, the queen loses herself, totally unaware of where she is. The cock inside her starts to grow again, the expansion greater than any previous one. The tendrils take firm hold of the soaked slippery walls, finding their footing despite the wetness. As the queen comes out of her haze, she realizes immediately that her cunt is completely stuffed. She realizes that there is again no escape as Remy's cock fucks her with little help from the elf. She wants to be close to him again but his thick serpent needs to first do its thing. It does, and then Remy wills his cock shorter again. As the cock shortens, the queen takes firm hold of the man. Despite her exhaustion, the queen settles into another orb deposit, bracing for the explosion. She manages three more explosions before she hands the elf over to her accompanying fairies so that they can see the elf through the twelve hours of fucking needed to satisfy him. It's the least she can do after all since she started this fire. The queen is attended to and once recovered, she enjoys the show.

ABOUT THE AUTHOR

Mackenzie Harnden is an emerging erotica author of many erotica kinks and sub-genres. Be sure to check out other books and leave a review if this story got you hot!

Visit my blog at Mackenzie Harnden Blog

Join my newsletter for exclusive Mackenzie Harnden Newsletter

Sign up for Free Stories from Xplicit Press Authors

Xplicit Press Author UpdatesShon Gacy Newsletter

Like Xplicit Press on Facebook

Follow Xplicit Press on Twitter

Readers: I want to expand a few of the stories to see where the characters can be explored further. If there are any of the stories that you would like to read more about again, I'd love to hear from you!

Keep In Touch
Mackenzie Harnden
info@mackenzieharnden.com